Dreamstones

Story by Maxine Trottier
Paintings by Stella East

Stoddart
Kids
TORONTO • NEW YORK

to the memory of Jan Helms,
mariner, adventurer, and friend
— M. T.

for the Inuit and their homeland
— S. E.

Art provided in the captain's notebook is by Jan-Kåre Øien

Published in Canada in 1999 by
Stoddart Kids,
a division of Stoddart Publishing Co. Limited
34 Lesmill Road
Toronto, Canada M3B 2T6
Tel (416) 445-3333 Fax (416) 445-5967
E-mail cservice@genpub.com

Distributed in Canada by
General Distribution Services
325 Humber College Blvd.
Toronto, Canada M9W 7C3
Tel (416) 213-1919 Fax (416) 213-1917
E-mail cservice@genpub.com

Published in the United States in 2000 by
Stoddart Kids,
a division of Stoddart Publishing Co. Limited
180 Varick Street, 9th Floor
New York, New York 10014
Toll free 1-800-805-1083
E-mail gdsinc@genpub.com

Distributed in the United States by
General Distribution Services, PMB 128
4500 Witmer Industrial Estates
Niagara Falls, New York 14305-1386
Toll free 1-800-805-1083
E-mail gdsinc@genpub.com

04 03 02 01 00   2 3 4 5 6

Canadian Cataloguing in Publication Data

Trottier, Maxine
Dreamstones

ISBN 0-7737-3191-1 (bound)   ISBN 0-7737-6141-1 (pbk.)

I. East, Stella. II. Title.

PS8589.R685D73 2000   jC813'.54   C99-930793-2
PZ7.T66Dr 2000

A captain's son becomes separated from his icebound ship,
and in doing so, becomes part of the mystique surrounding
the striking stone figures the Inuit call Inukshuks.

Visit Maxine's web-site at www.execulink.com/~maxitrot/maxine.htm

THE CANADA COUNCIL | LE CONSEIL DES ARTS
FOR THE ARTS | DU CANADA
SINCE 1957 | DEPUIS 1957

We acknowledge for their financial support of our publishing
program the Canada Council, the Ontario Arts Council, and
the Government of Canada through the Book Publishing
Industry Development Program (BPIDP).

Printed and bound in Hong Kong, China by
Book Art Inc., Toronto

It was early one spring when
the *Lily* sailed from England.
It was summer when her anchor
dropped into a bay far to the north.
Her captain said to his son, "This will
be a fine place to study the creatures
that live here, David." And he was right.

Nesting birds swam and squabbled everywhere. Caribou and Arctic foxes crisscrossed the vast land. While the captain drew the animals, David wandered the beach, collecting pebbles and bits of bone. He watched birds lift into the air, blocking out the sun as the ship's crew worked on the deck to prepare the *Lily* for her voyage home.

Sometimes he walked inland with his father. On the hills in the distance, strange figures of rock rose against the cold, blue sky. "Those are markers to lead you home," the captain told his son. "People here call them *Inukshuks*. They say some are as old as time."

David wondered at the lichen-covered stones stacked in human shapes. He had seen the people of this land. Wrapped in fur clothing, they looked like the Inukshuks that watched on the hills.

One night there was a ring around the moon. The next day the wind shifted. A storm blew in and when it ended three days later, the ship was held fast in ice. The *Lily* had stayed too long.

Now everyone remained on board most of the time. The wind howled and sounds of ice pressing against the hull groaned around them. Once, echoing through the ship, they heard the far-off song of whales under the sea. Each day was colder, each night was longer, until finally the sun did not rise at all and the

One night when winter had gone on forever, and none of them had seen the sun for so very long, a sound woke David. He turned in his bed and looked out of the port. A curl of moon, bowed and silvery, hung like a lantern in the sky. A million stars glittered. He heard the sound again. A sharp, quick barking of foxes rang in the night.

David pulled on his coat and hurried up the ladder. Below, his father and the crew slept on. There at the edge of the shore, two foxes stood in the moonlight. David climbed down the gangplank and ran across the frozen bay. For a moment he saw the foxes' laughing, black eyes. The animals turned and scampered over the snow, stopping just at the edge of a hill.

"They want to play," David thought as he followed, the foxes dancing just out of reach. Puffs of white drifted from their small, black noses. The ship's mast disappeared in the darkness. At last David stopped. Behind him, the *Lily* was gone. Ahead, the foxes melted into the night. He was alone.

David wandered up one hill and down the other, but everything looked the same. Then he heard a voice.

"Are you lost?" called someone. At the top of the hill stood a man.

"Yes!" David shouted back. "Can you show me the way?" David walked toward him. The man was tall and broad, dressed in grey fur that ruffled in the wind. A hood shadowed his face. His fur mukluks were planted solidly on the snowy ground.

"It would be best to wait until the sun rises," said the man.

"The sun has disappeared," answered David. "It has been night for so long."

"Ah, but this is a special night," said the man. "This is the night the sun comes back. If you are patient, you will see it."

So David waited.

The man had wood, boards from an old whaling ship he said, and he made a fire. Flames danced over the frozen ground and snapping sparks licked the darkness. David sat near the heat, wrapped in the man's fur robes. All night they watched, and as they watched they talked. David told the man about the *Lily* and his father and the creatures they had seen. The man told David secrets about the animals and what they dreamed.

"All things dream here," he said. "Even the sleeping stones."

"I dream of going home," said David quietly. "What do you dream?"

"I dream of the sun," answered the man and he pointed to the sky.

David looked up from the fire. At the very edge of the earth the golden rim of the sun rose. For just a moment it sat there, rich and warm in that cold place.

"It's back," whispered David sleepily.

The man said nothing. He only stared at the horizon as the sun briefly touched his smiling face.

When the captain discovered that his son was gone, he
and the crew lit torches and set out into the dark. Some
of the northern people walked with them. They found David
wrapped in grey sealskin, asleep near the glowing embers
of a fire. Behind him stood the Inukshuk, against which
he had taken shelter.

Each day after that the sun stayed a little longer. The nights became shorter. One night there was a ring around the moon. The next day the wind shifted and a storm blew in. When it ended three days later, the *Lily* had broken free from the thin ice. Spring had come back to the North.

The *Lily's* great anchor was raised from the ocean floor, the crew unfurled the sails, and the ship headed out to sea. It was never seen again.

Some winters when
the night is long and
still, the old people tell a
story. In it, there is a ship and
a boy and a tall stone figure. The
children's eyes widen when they hear
of how the Inukshuk walked that one,
special night. They shiver in their beds
just a little. But then they sleep and
dream. For all things dream here, even the
sleeping stones.

Author's Note

Inukshuk (ee-nook-shook) is an Inuktitut word that means "to look like a person". These striking figures of piled rocks were sometimes called the compasses of the Arctic. Today, Inukshuks are still used by hunters and travelers throughout the Far North. In a place where people have always had close ties to the land and each other, the Inukshuk is a symbol of friendship.